GREZIA,
The Brave Red Knight

ANDRE CABRA
Illustrator: Ana Luisa Peralta Villalobos

To order additional copies of this book, contact:
Xlibris
844-714-8691
www.Xlibris.com
Orders@Xlibris.com

ISBN: Softcover   978-1-6641-9541-7
         Hardcover   978-1-6641-9542-4
         EBook   978-1-6641-9540-0

Library of Congress Control Number: 2021921987

Print information available on the last page

Rev. date: 10/29/2021

Eastern Rosa

Grezia is the daughter of a very brave Knight. She also lives with her brother, Luke. One day, they were hunting with in the forest and saw a gentle deer drinking from the river. Grezia wants to pet the deer but is too scared to get close to it.

"Look at these delicious humans. You're mine now!" A gigantic gray snake appears behind them opening it's gigantic mouth with lots of sharp teeth.

Grezia's father points his bow to the gigantic snake protecting Grezia and Luke. Leave us alone hideous beast!, her father demands. Grezia begins crying, "Daddy, daddy, I'm scared!"

A Knight with bright and shiny armor riding his majestic horse appears from the woods and jumps in to save them. The Red Knight strikes his sword injuring the gigantic snake on the tail forcing it to run away.

Grezia's eyes sparkled as the Red Knight defeated the gigantic snake. From that day she said to herself, "I will be as brave as the brave Red Knight." The Red Knight disappears into the distance.

Back home in their village, Grezia follows her brother Luke, who is training to become a Knight along with his friends. She wants to train with them but they all laugh at her.

"Hahaha... You can't be a Knight. You're just a scared little girl."

They challenge her to spend one night alone in the dangerous forest outside of the village.

"But the forest is very dangerous. Especially at night," Grezia replies shakily.

Luke smirks at her, "Just go home. You will never be a knight."

Grezia raises her chin and chest with courage, "I'll show you how brave I am. I'll be as brave as the brave Red Knight."

As soon as the moon shines the night, they all leave her alone in the forest. Grezia hugs herself near a fire her brother had helped her ignite. She begins to hear the animal noises inside the forest that make her panic.

She begins imagining all kinds of scary things like skeletons creeping out of the woods and snakes slithering around the grass.

Grezia tears up and cuddles herself tightly until morning when the sun comes up.

"I"ll be as brave as the brave Red Knight", she says to herself.

Grezia wakes up to the bright sun in the morning and sees a little green snake on the ground. Without a thought, she jumps up screaming and runs away deeper into the forest.

"Daddy, daddy, I'm scared!"

She stops running and realizes she ran too far. "Oh no, how do I get back?"

She sees the river flowing harshly down stream. "Daddy always said that if I follow the river, I'll find my way back to the village"

Grezia keeps walking further and sees three horses nearby. A black, a white and a gray horse drinking from the river. "I'll show them how brave I am. The Red Knight has a horse. I need a horse too.", she gulps facing her fear.

Grezia slowly approaches the horses little by little. She hesitates every step she takes taking deep breaths. "I'm as brave as the brave Red Knight"

As soon as she gets close enough, "NEEEEEIIIIIIGHH"

The black horse lets out a powerful neigh rising on its two hooves. Grezia drops to the ground and closes her eyes. "Aaaaaah! Daddy, I'm scared! I'm scared of the black horse!"

The black horse starts sniffing her. She opens her eyes seeing the black horse right on top of her casting a shadow. Grezia trembles in fear. The black horse lowers it's nose smelling Grezia.

"I'll be as brave as the Red Knight.", she whispers herself. She looks up at the horse and puts her hand slowly and gently on his nose. "Do you want to ride with me?," she asks the horse.

The black horse lifts her up to it's back. "I'll show them how brave I am. I'll call you Lu, short for Luke."

Lu and Grezia stop at the cliff of a mountain. "I can see our home across the river. It looks really scary. I should find something to protect myself. The Red Knight has armor to protect himself. I need armor too."

They arrive at the riverbed when Grezia sees a huge tree with branches spreading all over the vast forest.
"I'll make my armor from this tree."

"You most certainly
won't, little girl!"

A mouth and eyes open up from the tree.

Grezia breaks out in a panic. "The huge tree just
talked! I'm scared, I'm scared!"
The tree laughs a rusty aged laugh,
"There's nothing to worry about little
girl. Don't be scared. But I won't let you
cut my roots."

"I wasn't scared", she whines and lies. "I'll be
as brave as the brave Red Knight. But how will
I get armor to protect me?"

"This is a very dangerous forest. You definitely need something to protect you.", the huge tree says, "I have an armor with magical powers. It will protect you wherever you go."

The huge tree opens it's mouth wide showing a bright and shining red armor inside of him.

"But be careful. Only the bravest of the bravest can wear this armor. If you are not brave, the magic will not work and the armor will get weak and break. Only one other brave knight before you has been able to wear this red armor"

She lifts her chin up high and raises her chest. "I'll show you how brave I am. I'll be as brave as the brave Red Knight."

She goes through the huge tree's mouth and puts on the armor. "I am as brave as the brave Red Knight!"

"Thank you for the armor. By the way, do you know how to cross the river?", she asks the tree.

"Hmm, crossing the river won't be easy. A gigantic snake slithers around the river."
"A gigantic snake?!", fears Grezia, "I'm scared. I'm scared of the gigantic snake."

A piece of the armor cracks as she panics. "The armor broke!"

The huge tree exclaims, "Remember, if you are not brave enough, the magic in the armor will get weak. Are you sure you can handle it?"

Grezia crosses her arms. "I'll show you how brave I am. I'll be as brave as the Red Knight."

She mounts Lu heading to the river. "I hope we don't run into the gigantic snake. My sword and shield broke so now I need to find another one."

Grezia reaches the river. "It'll be dangerous to cross the river."

She sees the river flowing really fast and harsh.

"Well what have we here?", The water rising and splashing everywhere as the gigantic snake emerges from the water.

She turns around, Aaah! The gigantic snake! I'm scared, I'm scared!

"You won't get away this time little girl." The gigantic snake laughs at her.

"I'm scared! I'm scared of the gigantic snake!" New cracks appear on her shiny armor.

Lu charges as fast as the wind through the trees but the gigantic snake blocks the path with its long body. "You can't run away from me little girl."

As Lu is forced to stop hastily, Grezia falls off Lu.

"No where to run little girl," The gigantic snake laughs.
"Bwahahahaha," the gigantic snake can't stop laughing. "I'll eat you and your horse.
If only you were brave enough to face me."

Grezia takes a deep breath and remembers what the tree told her, This armor will
protect me as long as I am brave.
She lifts her chin up and raises her chest, "I'll show you how brave I am. I'll be as
brave as the brave Red Knight," she yells to the gigantic snake facing her fear.

With it's sharp teeth, the gigantic snake plunges at Grezia ready to eat when...
CLINK!!!!!!!

"AAAAAAH!!"
Her bravery makes the armor fill with its magical power making it impenetrable. The gigantic snake's teeth all shatter into pieces as he charged for the bite.

"My armor! It protected me! I knew I was as brave as the Red Knight!"

The gigantic snake cries and cries. "My teeth! It hurts!" Grezia picks up one of the snake's tooth. As soon as she picks it up, her bright shiny red armor uses its magic to transform the tooth into her new sword."I'll make my sword from this tooth."

She pokes the snake with her new sword made out of the gigantic snake's poisonous tooth. The gigantic snakes faints unconscious.
"I am as brave as the brave red knight. Let's get back home Lu."

Grezia and Lu finally get back home. "I can't wait to explore the forest again! I bet my daddy and brother are worried about me. I'll tell them that I am as brave as The Brave Red Knight!"

The End

Printed in the United States
by Baker & Taylor Publisher Services